MW01268384

Irish Mystery Stories

by Michael Surmont

Copyright © 2012 Michael Surmont

All rights reserved.

ISBN: 1480142913
ISBN:978-1480142916

First Edition: September 2012

This is a work of fiction. Names, characters, places, and incidents either are products of the author's imagination or are used fictitiously. Any resemblance to actual events, locales, or persons, living or dead, is entirely coincidental.

All rights reserved. No part of this publication can be reproduced or transmitted in any form or by any means without permission in writing from Author.

To Noreen

CONTENTS

Book 1: The Child in Black

Introduction 1
Chapter I 2
Chapter II 5
Chapter III 8
Final 11

Book 2: The Voice

Introduction 15
Chapter I 16
Chapter II 20
Chapter III 22
Chapter IV 24
Chapter V 25
Chapter VI 28
Chapter VII 30
Chapter VIII 32
Chapter IX 34
Chapter X 36
Chapter XI 38
Final 40

Book 3: On the Third Day

Chapter I 45
Chapter II 48
Chapter III 51

About the Author 57

Irish Mystery Stories

The Child in Black

INTRODUCTION

I can't remember when I first visited Turlaur Abbey; but I do know that it was not at that time when I developed such a fear of this mysterious place. This began a few years later; the day the legend became a reality before my eyes... the day I saw *"the child in black"*.

CHAPER I

"The Child in Black" is an old Irish legend of County Wicklow that my grandfather used to tell my brothers and myself in the long cold winter evenings; even though many attested to the veracity of the story, I would never have imagined that I would witness it for myself.

It all happened on a grey, wet morning in the autumn of 1983; I was only 8 years old at the time, and like every Sunday I woke up before my brothers to go with my mother to visit the grave of my grandfather at the cementery of the abbey.

Turlaur Abbey is only two miles from our home; it is an abandoned and ruined medieval monastery anchored at one edge of Turlaur Lake, in the heart of County Wicklow.

A long time ago it was a glorious Dominican monastery; but of all its former glory only a temple of silence and oblivion remain; where the sound of the voices of its past inhabitants have been replaced by the quietness of the local cemetery; with headstones surrounding the now ruined and still abbey, giving it an aura of mystery and reverence.

Sometimes I like to imagine what this place was like in its glory days; when it was full of monks, visitors and animals; when the roof of the church was still intact and would have housed dozens of parishioners who met there every Sunday to celebrate mass.

Right now I could hear their voices and their laughter; the murmur of prayer in the dark, gloomy temple; the slow steps of an old monk climbing the steep stairway towards the bell tower... Nothing remains of all that now. Today from the top of its bell-less tower the only sound to be heard is the deafening echoes of the whistling wind; and the only roof now visible is the sky itself. Contemplating its ruins awakens in me feelings of melancholy and nostalgia, peace and transcendence ... inquietude.

Granddad had died a year ago and like most of the older locals in the area he was buried in the graveyard next to the abbey ruins. Every Sunday my mother and I would put flowers on his grave as a gesture from us all to say we had not forgotten him.

When we arrived we found the usual scenario;

the place was totally deserted; there was an impenetrable silence which was only broken by the monotonous melody of the rain and the eternal moan of the Irish wind.

My mother opened the old iron-gate; the creaking of its rusty hinges frightened a few birds; just a tiny robin remained looking curiously over the headstone of an old tomb.

"The soul of a child", I said, pointing at the bird, who watching us did not appear bothered by our presence. My mother smiled and continued walking.

Granddad's grave was outside the temple, just behind the apse; it was in this section of the cemetery where the most recent graves were placed. We walked along what was once the wall of the central nave of the church.

I already knew the task that followed; my mother removed the old and withered flowers and with a small cotton cloth, cleaned the jar that contained them; once clean, she passed it to me to fill with fresh water. The best place for this task was the stone pier over the lake at the other side of the abbey; the pier extended just a few feet above the lake, and due to its low altitude it was the easiest place to reach the surface of the water.

CHAPTER II

Taking a shortcut through the interior of the church, I approached the lake passing under the *"Angel's Gate"*; a small side door of the nave that had been given this name because of an almost unnoticed small figure of an angel carved into its top frame. From this door I had to walk no more than forty steps to reach the pier; passing through this doorway I could not help but stop for a moment to observe the image of the angel. The little figure was graceful and simple, and though his face had disappeared with the passing of time, it was still possible to recognize his wings; his right hand raised in a gesture of blessing; and a mysterious key in his left hand. The size of the key was well out of proportion with the small size of the angel; no doubt whoever sculpted this wanted to emphasize the importance of that element.

Without knowing why, I extended my hand to touch the key; it was perhaps one of those challenges so typical of childhood, done with the sole purpose of trying to overcome a height or a distance with one's own body. I don't know why I did it, but what I do remember is that at that precise instant when the tips of my fingers touched the cold and porous stone, a hustled but clearly audible noise raced past my back; It resembled steps, running away in a hurry, making the leaves rustle on its way.

Frightened I turned at once, but all I found was the bleak image of the inside of the church, that with its high grey walls without a roof to cover them, resembling a desolated labyrinth of a giant.

"Birds...", I thought nervously, and quickly went on my way.

That strange noise had awakened my imagination and dozens of figures began to dance through my mind; I thought of a little elf, of the many who inhabit this Emerald Isle; who had probably followed me closely and then ran away when it feared it might be discovered. I also imagined a group of crows that may have hid under dry leaves, who were frightened by my presence and took flight precipitously ... I imagined a huge rat that was going to devour me!

Fleeting and fantastic explanations came to mind with neither order nor reason; one more absurd than the other; but I avoided the explanation that would have scared me more than any of the others; the one that Granddad had told us so many times and the one I had almost completely forgotten: The child in Black!

Once on the pier, the noises and ideas that had occurred to me only seconds before were completely forgotten and I was ready to collect the water.

CHAPTER III

The lake lay before me as a peaceful sight covered by a thick, impenetrable grey curtain of fog that hardly allowed me a glimpse of the other side.

I positioned myself face down with my body completely stretched over the pier and my arms and head hanging over the edge; humming an old Irish tune I began to fill the jar

The water was freezing cold and crystal clear; so clear in fact that I was able to see my own reflection.

There over the pier was where I first witnessed the after-life, my first contact with the world of the unknown, of the inexplicable; that world we can not understand nor explain ... but it is here; it exists.

After filling the jar and removing it from the water, I kept watching my reflection on the surface of the lake. It was hypnotizing as I allowed myself to experience the drowsy effect the water had on me. I watched as my image floated on the surface; it rocked gently, fractionating into dozens of pieces as if I was looking into a broken mirror. The sound of the small blows of the water against the pier were like the soft tick-tock of an antique clock, a rhythmic, soothing music, which invited the imagination to be transported to a world different from our own.

The movement of the waves became slower and slower and as the water was recovering its calm, my image began to regain its shape and integrity.

I would have stayed there for much longer, absorbed and contemplative; when at the very precise moment when the lake surface completely calmed, I saw behind my shoulder a face smiling back at me.

I jumped up and turned at once, I wanted to scream but I couldn't; greater was my surprise when all that was visible before me was the pier, completely deserted; only a few meters from me, the old and quiet abbey was watching from the distance. Its high stone walls were standing thirty feet from where I was; between them and myself was only a blanket of silence ... nothing else; but as soon as I raised my eyes toward the bell tower I could see her figure completely intact throughout the years; there she was! She stood as straight and still as the abbey itself; completely motionless at the window of the bell tower wearing her long, old black dress; as pale and silent as the moon; perfect and unblemished as time. There she was… watching me with a serious expression on her face, her long black hair and old clothes swaying in the wind.

"The child in black!", I exclaimed bringing both hands to my mouth to quiet a cry of horror.

My heart was beating so hard, I could almost hear it in the stillness of the moment; there she stood staring at me, smiling…

The story that Granddad had told us so many times in the past crossed my mind in a second and a shiver ran through my entire body; she was just as he had described! ... And there she was now ... watching me from the top of the abbey!

Still today I can not say how long I was there; how long it took me to collect the jar that had fallen on the pier, nor how fast I ran to my mother and left that mysterious place ... I only know that it seemed like an eternity, every second like a year; every minute, a century.

FINAL

I have not returned to Turlaur Abbey since. The image of the child in black still awakes me in the long winter nights; I imagine her standing there in the bell tower, with her porcelain white face that does not age; as time passes she continues to stand there looking down at me while her long dark hair and her old black dress gently sway in the breeze.

The Voice

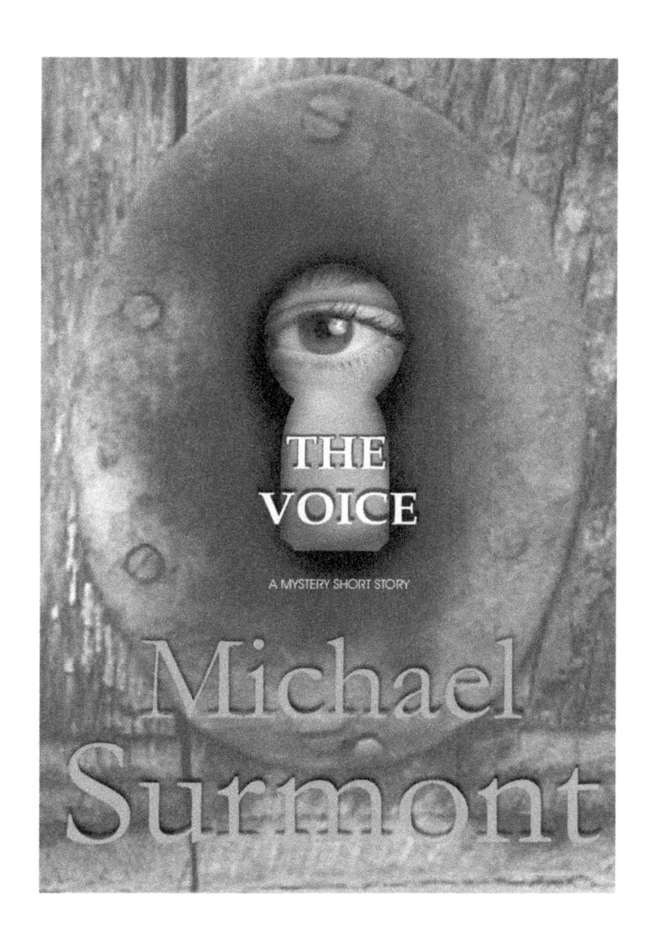

INTRODUCTION

"I do not like the music classroom... the musty smell of the worn wooden floor; the out of tune notes from the battered upright piano; old mouldy glass windows that transforms the beautiful sunlight into a surreal atmosphere; walls that mutely bear witness to my loneliness... mistakes from the past that have my name etched all over them... memories that fade with the passing of time ... I hate this class! I hate this place!
But still I know that I have to love it... I must love it with all my heart because it is right here where it all began and where everything will possibly end; it is in this lonely part of the school where that afternoon my senses perceived that mysterious world that is right here beside us... that distant afternoon when I heard what I should not have heard, when I opened the door I should never have opened....

CHAPTER I

It was a Thursday afternoon; like any other Thursday we were condemned to one of the worst torments that students of Terenure College would have to face: complete boredom in music class while Mr. Grafton played all those horrible tunes on the piano, which we were forced to sing along to at school acts.

Mr. David Grafton was a very good teacher; he had that peculiar distracted character that musicians and many other artists so often have; which can be amusing for students to watch. But every time we were in the music room this meek side of his turned dramatically irritable and a darkness surfaced that became visibly more evident. It was as if somebody else stepped into his body; it seemed as if that mysterious classroom was hiding a dark and sinister force capable of transforming Mr. Grafton's good and patient heart into a completely cold and irritable one.

Like every Thursday after lunch-time the class began at two o'clock, and there were my classmates and me; well, I'd rather say I was not completely there; because while my body was sitting at my desk, repeating mechanically the song that Mr. Grafton was trying to teach us; my mind was wandering elsewhere to places far more interesting than music class.

The out of tune piano projected its music throughout the air once and once again like the monotonous and repetitive talk of a drunkard. At the other corner of the room, fat Carsey Roger was yawning ad nauseum, opening his big fat mouth as if he was going to swallow the whole class, piano included. I smiled watching him, he was as vulgar as ever. I was about to yawn myself when suddenly I heard someone whispering my name.

It was a weak but sharp voice that came from someone sitting to my right; I immediately looked at James Towey; he was usually lost at this point as to where we were with the lyrics, and he regularly asked me to help him out; but this time I was surprised to see that James was completely focused, reviewing his lyrics as he sang horribly out of tune and extremely loud; I think he was the only one of the entire class that afternoon who seemed to like that tedious melody.

My thoughts were still occupied with this when I heard my name again. This time the voice was much more audible; it was now hoarse and I was quite sure that it was coming from beside the door, where *"Redhead"* McGuire was sitting.

Everything suddenly became very clear! Seamus McGuire loved practical jokes like whispering someone´s name and imitating different funny voices; so that when you turned to ask him what he wanted, he completely ignored you and behaved as if nothing had happened; and sometimes, and this was his aim; Mr. Grafton would reproach you, thinking it was you who was trying to disrupt the class.

"Redhead" McGuire was visibly more bored than the rest of us; and even though he was pretending to read his lyrics, I was quite sure it was he who had been calling me from the beginning; I could have even sworn that I glimpsed that half mocking grin he used to wear on his lips when he was up to some mischief.

The piano stopped playing and Mr. Grafton began to flip through his notebook looking for a new song to teach us. Seizing the opportunity and forgetting McGuire for the moment, I raised my hand and asked to go to the bathroom; it was a permission that Mr. Grafton never refused; and an excellent excuse to leave class and take a "short tour" of the school; avoiding of course an unpleasant encounter with Ms. Wilson, our feared principal who used to pound through the school, taking students out of their classes for meaningless interrogations.

Given the positive affirmation from Mr. Grafton I jumped up and crossed the room to leave class at once; but not before on the sly giving McGuire a quick flick with the tip of my index finger to the back of his head. McGuire gasped, took both hands to his head and tried to get me with a kick.

I dodged it, closing the door behind me while I listened to the voice of Mr. Grafton reprimanding McGuire for his violent outburst; Ah! Those words were music to my ears! I could not help but laugh imagining the foolish look of surprise that "Redhead" McGuire would etch on his face as he always did when teachers chastised him; an event that occurred quite often indeed.

CHAPTER II

I was now outside the class; Mr. Grafton had started a new song and the notes of the piano filtered in a muffled manner through the old wooden door with its opaque glass. All the class were now bored, everyone that is except me! I was free like the wind! The school was mine!

However, before I had even time to take a step, I could hear that voice again, calling out my name. I could not help but being startled this time; the voice sounded as if its owner had sighed my name in my ear... and then I heard something like the fading sound of children´s laughter and footsteps running away.

In the small hall where I was now standing there were just three doors; the door that leads to the music room and which I had just closed a few seconds ago; the door that communicates the hallway with the other classrooms and the toilets where I was going to; and that mysterious wood and glass panelled door which was always locked and where it was only possible to see an impenetrable darkness.

A chill ran through my entire body; because without being able to explain how or why, I was quite sure that the voice and laughter came from behind that door.

CHAPTER III

Among the students many myths circulated as to what was locked behind that mysterious door. Some of the more imaginative kids would say that it led to a secret section of the school where the Principal would lock herself into on full moon nights to become a werewolf. Other students certainly no less fanciful, asserted that behind the dirty glass of the door hid the ghost of a monk who had burned alive at the school over a century ago, and whose apparition roamed these halls at night. Finally, the more reasonable ones affirmed that the room was only used as storage for old desks and other useless belongings of the school.

Like any myth that is created and fed by the imagination of the children of a school; it grows and becomes more powerful simply because it can never be proven; and in the case of the mysterious door this simply happened because the door was always locked. Many had tried in vain to open it; and the teachers never responded when we asked what was inside.

While all these myths were fusing together in my mind, the voice repeated my name once again; if I was absorbed in my thoughts up to this point, his tone, now a categorical and imperative shout, leapt me out of them with a feeling of complete and utter fear.

This time I didn´t hear laughter, but now I was completely sure that the voice was coming from behind the door.

Without dubitation I extended my hand and firmly took the brass handle; it was cold. I knew that it would be useless trying to turn it because the door was always locked... but I took my chances ... and the unthinkable happened; unfortunately for me, the handle turned and with a creaking noise the door opened.

CHAPTER IV

I found myself facing a dreadful dilemma; as I was a reasonable individual, I could have renounced to the mysteries and perhaps dangers that were hidden in there, and turning myself around I would have returned immediately to music class, or simply continued on my way to the toilets; but as childhood is the first cousin of curiosity, and also of pride; pride in that I immediately thought of the esteem and admiration everyone would feel for me, by just knowing that I was the first to enter the "forbidden room", a nickname by the way, “Redhead” McGuire had christened the place; I decided I was going to check it out! I took a deep breath, braced myself... and walked in.

CHAPTER V

I closed the door behind me. I remember the place smelled like my grandmother's house; a mixture of wet wood and chicken broth. The lighting was poor but I could see that the room was big. To my right I glimpsed two huge windows boarded up with large wooden slats that allowed only faint rays of light to filter through. Gradually my eyes adapted to the semi-darkness and I began to distinguish the shapes of almost everything that was around me.

The place seemed to have been used as a classroom many years ago. There were old desks ordered in rows transverse to the door where I stood; some had fallen and others were covered with old, once white sheets. To my left, just where the desks were facing, I noticed what would have been the teacher's desk; and hanging over the dark wall behind it I recognized the silhouette of a huge, old black board. Everything was covered with years of layers of dust and decades of silence.

I had seen enough, something about that place frightened me to the core and I decided I had sufficient information to impress my friends and the entire school.

Suddenly, I realized that the voice I had heard before was now completely silent; and for some self convincing reason I assumed that all I had heard minutes before was just a product of my imagination; that the room was only an abandoned section of the school and there was nothing to fear... as many a student had said, the place was just a simple storage for old furniture and there was no such thing as principal werewolves or ghostly monks… even so these ideas did not completely reassure me, nor less calm me down; and with no further dubitation I decided to leave the room at once.

I was about to turn around when my eyes glimpsed something written on the blackboard; it was a single sentence probably written in white chalk; and although the letters were big enough, it was impossible to read it from where I was standing because of the lack of proper lighting. There were about five steps from the door to the blackboard; it would only take me seconds to get there, read it, and run out of the place. With big steps, courageously I approached the board to read the message someone must have written many decades ago.

CHAPTER VI

If I was nervous or a little scared before; it was nothing, absolutely nothing compared to the deep sense of terror I felt when I read what was written on the blackboard.

It is amazing how many thoughts can pass through one´s mind in an instant, in less than a second. The whirlwind of ideas that enters the head of someone who is in an extreme situation as the one I was in, is simply indescribable; and how all these different and confusing ideas arrive at a single and powerful conclusion in a matter of seconds, is practically a mystery; but it happens, and very often.

In the few seconds it took me to run from that room, only one conclusion lit up inside my head like a light that suddenly shines at the end of a long black tunnel; everything seemed to me as clear as water and I felt completely foolish. I was sure I had been the victim of a dark prank of "Redhead" McGuire´s.

CHAPTER VII

McGuire knew that like every Thursday during music, I would raise my hand and ask Mr. Grafton if I could go to the bathroom; he also knew that Mr. Grafton would not refuse, and once out of the class I would have to pass through the small hall with the three doors. With all this information McGuire then did the following: during class he called me by my name to confuse and arouse my curiosity; then, when I left to go to the bathroom, he waited until I was in the hall and then managed to keep whispering my name from inside the music room through the door, with the intention that I would believe that the voice was coming from the "forbidden room"; he surely knew before music class that the mysterious door was open; for some lucky reason he had discovered it, and knowing that I would bite the hook, open the door, go into the abandoned classroom, and read the board; he simply came in earlier and with the intention of scaring me, he wrote the words on the blackboard that I would later read:

"They will never see you again"

I felt very sure of the conclusion I had reached; and even though I was furious with McGuire´s prank, I had to admit that his plan had worked since I left that room ten times faster than I had entered it.

I closed the door insulting "Redhead" almost in a shout as I did so; I was thinking of returning to the music room to hit him before he had the chance of laughing at me... but all my anger was gone when I turned and looked around the small hall; it was a real cold surprise... the real horror of my adventure was just about to begin.

CHAPTER VIII

Everything was dark, completely dark and quiet; the sun was replaced by the moon that shined through the windows… it was night!

I was shocked and confused; I knew it was absolutely impossible that in the few minutes I spent in the room for night to have fallen. When I left the music room, the afternoon was just beginning and there were still many hours until dusk… but the real fact was that I had entered the "forbidden room" during the afternoon and left it in the dark of night.

I tried to find an explanation; I thought maybe I had fallen asleep; but I knew that I hadn't. I couldn't understand what was happening. I remained completely motionless for a moment, listening to the silence of the empty and desolate school; suddenly, a huge distress began to burn inside me and I wished to be back home immediately.

I tried to open the music room but the door was locked; the lights were out and I couldn't hear anyone inside.

I then opened the door that leads into the corridor and started to walk. The moon light was filtering through the side windows. In my confusion I was trying to control my fear but with little success; the fear instead was beginning to take control of me. I was walking slowly as if I was afraid of being heard; I knew that if Tim, the night watchman, found me here at this hour I would not have a good excuse to give him.

Suddenly, as I went further down the corridor, I noticed that at the other side of the playground the lights of the small school chapel were on; I assumed there was some type of celebration going on and I confirmed my thoughts when I saw a man, who appeared to arrive late, hurriedly open the door of the chapel and go inside.

I screamed at him waving my arms in order to get his attention, but he did not seem to hear me and disappeared behind the door.

Never the less, I felt relief knowing I was not alone; I crossed the playground as fast as I could until I got to the chapel door.

CHAPTER IX

When I opened the door the place was in complete silence; everybody was on their knees praying, and even the priest himself was inclined.

Almost all the heads present were grey; I supposed it surely was an ex-student's celebration, and probably a very old one at that; it was something quite usual in a school as old as ours.

I stood quietly at the back, waiting for the Mass to end, when I would relay what had happened to me and ask for help. Certainly they would not believe a single word, and I would get a good telling-off at home for disappearing all day and causing my parents upset. I was thinking how worried my mother would be when suddenly the priest made a sign and they all stood up.

I remember each word that the priest slowly enunciated as if it were today... he thanked all those present and blessed them ... but before doing this he sadly mentioned the reason for the Mass and prayed once again for the boy who had disappeared 55 years ago, and raising his hands he prayed for....

CHAPTER X

When I heard the priest mention my name I fell to my knees, I could not believe what I was hearing… the Mass was for me! For me who was missing 55 years!

I was momentarily overcome with a numbness and a deep sense of shock; it was not a dream from which I could wake up; I was fully conscious and awake; that afternoon I had entered the forbidden room and left it 55 years later.

While they were praying I jumped up and ran towards the altar screaming and asking them to pay me attention; I knew there would be confusion and they would probably take me for a boy who wanted to play a bad joke, but I didn't care; I yelled my name and explained that I did not understand what was happening but I was alive… I was there and alive!

CHAPTER XI

No-one took a bit of notice of me; not even a glance was returned. The Mass was over; I stood there bewildered as everyone passed me by. I was shouting, begging for someone to hear me; I even tried to grab somebody's arm, but my hands just caught air.

In the tired eyes of the parishioners I recognized the aged faces of many of my classmates; the big Roger Carsey, Robert Seamus McGuire, James Towey, Christian Walson, Timothy Waldron...

Everyone was gone and the doors were closed... I stood there perplexed; and as soon as the lights went off the silence of the night found me lying there in the loneliness of a mysterious world; a secret world which that Thursday afternoon, curious and innocent I had desecrated.

FINAL

I have lost count of the hours, days, years that I've been waiting to hear the voice again; the voice that woke me up from this long nightmare that I would never have chosen to dream.
Another class starts in the music room today; new kids and new teachers pass before my eyes.
The notes of an old song are played in the same antique piano; only it has remained the same during all this time; observing me in silence as seriously as a saint observes the sinner. With a wave of the teacher´s hand the children begin to sing a melody ... it's the same old melody I did not want to sing once... but ... hold on!... Do you hear what I hear?... Listen! ... It´s the voice! It´s the same voice calling me by my name! It is calling me again! I knew it! After all this time it has not forgotten

me!
Come, come with me and let´s walk together through that door! This time I do not want to go on my own ... come on ... do not stop ... the voice is calling!"

On the Third Day

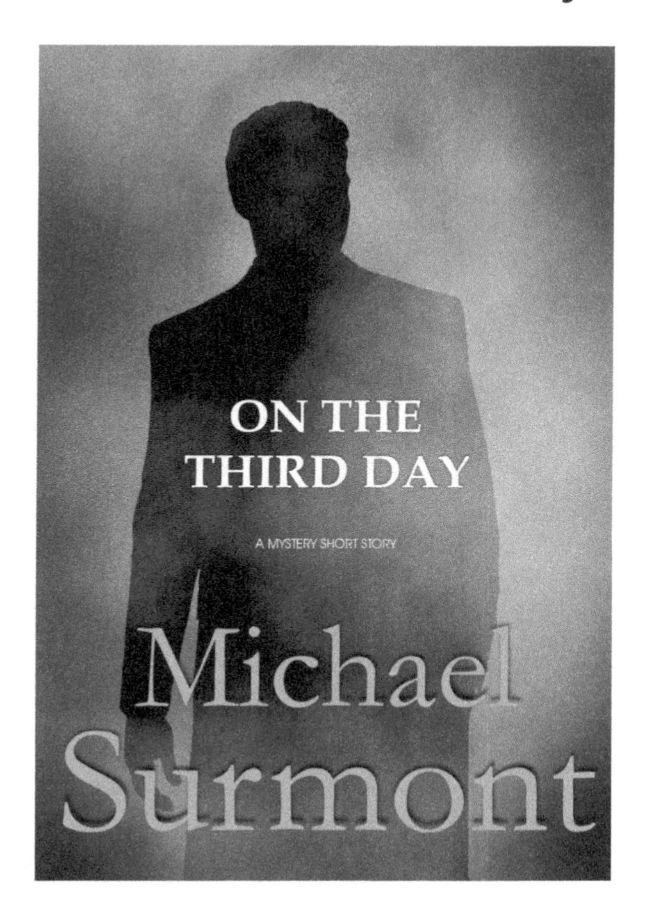

CHAPTER I

It was nearly six o'clock in the evening but the sun was still boasting the last of its weak rays across the grey clouds of the Dublin city skyline. It illuminated the last hours of what had been one of the dullest and coldest days of the now, near completed period of Lent, 1916.

The working day had ended for most; and within minutes, Grafton Street, the winding central street of the city's south-side, was already lit by yellowy hues of light emanating from the showcases that stood proudly either side of it. Bicycles and a few cars began to filter into the street alongside a compact crowd that populated both ends from Trinity College to beyond Stephen's Green. Alongside the tram stations nearby, workers neatly queued; those who lived closer to the centre simply walked to their homes.

Just a few minutes after the bells of Christ Church tolled The Angelus, the narrow streets of the centre were transformed into a dark and mysterious land, where the eternal rain and the tireless wind would be the only witnesses of its darker corners; a dark beer in the shelter of a pub would be the last refuge for most.

Everything seemed to indicate that we were facing a typical end of day; that slow and almost imperceptible rhythm in which the day mimics night and the city discreetly dresses in black; but this night would not be like any other; long before a new sun was born, a small group of men would witness a revolutionary event; something expected by many but perhaps disbelieved by most; a fact that would trigger bloody consequences; an act that would set a before and after in the history of mankind.

Those in the capital of the Emerald Isle would be protagonists that night of an event, completely unaware of their fate and barely capable of understanding their destiny; and if at that moment these men were sure of one thing, it was the simple fact that their names were echoed in the mouths and ears of all the authorities in the city; and that they would soon be indicted and pursued; and that from then on, the slightest slip could cost them their lives.

But let us leave this for later and return again to

the urban landscape of Grafton Street. There, under the timid lights of the shop windows and among the people, we can see one of these men, who with a hurried step walked towards an unknown destination.

CHAPTER II

The disturbed attitude of this man who stomped along Grafton Street would not go unnoticed by the eyes of a keen observer, who might even suggest that the fellow was not walking amongst the people, but was rather nervously breaking through them. His gait was quick and precise; suddenly he stopped and looked back in the distance as if he was afraid of being followed; after observing and standing completely still for a few seconds, he immediately resumed his march mingling amongst the crowd once again. It seemed as if he was carrying an important secret and the bulk of the Dublin authorities were chasing him with the one aim of catching and arresting him.

He was a thin, well-dressed man, wearing a

beige suede beret, black leather shoes, dark green, slightly worn-looking woollen trousers and a long coat that kept out the intense cold, in the pockets of which were hidden his hands.

Around his neck he wore a chain that held a small pendant with a Republican sign; something that in those days meant more than just a simple rebellious act.

A little further up, a scar was visible on his chin, it was probably the product of a wound recently received. He had a warm look which was framed in a hard-featured face partly obscured by a stubble of three days. His expression was of fear and worry; in his eyes was a glimmer of hope.

After passing by the portal of Trinity College he crossed the tram lines, and skirting the building of the Bank of Ireland he went towards City Hall; from there he walked the narrow cobbled streets of Templebar which led him to the riverside of the Liffey; quickly he crossed the Ha′Penny bridge, that arches gracefully over the river, from where he entered the dark streets of the north side of the city. Our mystery man was moving through the streets as if through a labyrinth; constantly changing direction and sometimes irrationally doubling back, and then returning to his previous route.

Although his walk appeared to be guided by a broken compass, it could be derived that he had a perfect knowledge of that part of the city in the certainty of his steps; and if at any time his path seemed unusual or misplaced, it would have been done with the express intent of misleading he who was hunting him. Finally, his mad race come to an end in a narrow, dark, and blind alley tucked away in some lost corner of the city's north side. There, illuminated by the dim light of an old lantern, was the door of one of the oldest pubs in the city; amongst the Republicans it was known as *"O'Regan's"*.

The mysterious man hesitated momentarily and then with an air of confidence braced himself and walked down the alley, stopping as he got to the door. Tired, breathless, and with his right foot already resting on the doorstep, he threw a last glance behind him. The murmur of the city whispered in the distant; and in the stillness of the narrow alley the only thing visible was a random cat who lay sleeping on top of a rubbish bag. The man sighed with relief; and without missing a second more he opened the door and walked in.

CHAPTER III

His nickname was *"The Twin"*, and he was the last of the squad to arrive at O'Regan's that evening. He looked pale and slightly shocked; beads of sweat sparkled like cold frost on his forehead. After closing the old oak door he stood for a moment and carefully scanned the faces of those present in the pub. The air smelled of a mixture of black beer and snuff. A quick glance gave him an exact idea of the place; near the entrance and around the bar counter was seated a large group of noisy workers; they were talking, joking, and laughing; intoxicated by an alcohol that had tinted their cheeks red. Beyond this group were some rustic wooden tables, placed without order, that stretched as far as the back of the pub; and right there, sitting around an old oak table beside the fireplace, away from the hustle and general merriment of the main crowd, sat the severe looking faces of the rest of the republican men; who waited restlessly and impatiently for his long overdue arrival and news.

"The twin" calmly smiled while acknowledging the group and seeing that everything was as they had agreed, approached them. They quietly greeted him with a barely perceptible nod. The beers on the table were almost full, and some of the men had not even taken a sip. Their faces were tired and fearful; the same fear that had chased "The twin" through the streets of Dublin a few minutes earlier.

Their names were already known by the authorities and they were well aware of that; the situation was grave.

- *Sorry for the delay* - he apologized, easing himself onto a chair.

After taking a sip of the beer that "The Taxman" offered him, he continued his speech, his words a bit broken at times from fatigue.

- *Someone recognized me, I was followed...*- he spluttered, - I had to change my route a few times until I lost him.

The men listened carefully as "The Twin" continued with his news.

- *I got the information ... from a good source.*

"Stone", the leader of the squad, moved his head closer to hear in detail what "The Twin" was about to reveal.

- *They saw him this morning!* – he whispered with

vigour – *He's alive!*

- *He's alive ...* – repeated "Stone"

A moment of joy dashing across the face of "Stone"; but suddenly he doubted his own words, lowered his head, and looked melancholically into the bottom of his glass.

- *Is this true?* - questioned "The Older" frowning.

- *But it's impossible...* - whispered "The Young", who could not hide his disbelief – *I've seen how they killed him! I saw him die with my own eyes!*

They were all deeply affected by the news brought by "The Twin"; three days ago the main leader of the revolution had been captured by the authorities and accused of being a rebel and traitor; after a prosecution without justice he was executed. The fear, that had harnessed the group a moment ago, seemed to dissipate amongst some on hearing the news. However, across the table confusion reigned alongside euphoria and hope; mixed emotions of shock and excitement were etched on their faces, as if they had forgotten the dangers that had preoccupied them seconds before.

"Stone", who was the most skeptical of them all, asked everyone to calm down until more accurate news was available.

- *I agree with "Stone"...* - said "The Twin" - *... I believe that this could be a trap.*

Soon what little enthusiasm there was before now seemed to slowly and reluctantly ebb away, seriousness quickly returning to their faces.

- *Maybe it is a trap, maybe...* - said "The Taxman"

stroking his beard thoughtfully …

- *Yes, it certainly could be...* – said "Stone" with some force behind his words - *...but if it is a trap it can only work if we believe it!*

- *Yes, I think so too,* - added "The Young" - *They want us to believe it, to give us a feeling of power again so that we will naively come out of our confinement...*

- *... and catch us and kill us like lambs* - added "Stone".

- *We must be cautious* - interjected "The Twin" – *There are women out there who say that they have seen Him ... but if I do not see Him with my own eyes ... I will not believe it!*

The echo of these last words were still hanging in the air when something unexpected happened; with the pub doors and windows closed and without being noticed by the group who were distracted with their discussion; the person who was the motive of their words walked directly to their table; His presence frightened them as if they were in the presence of a ghost. A deep silence fell upon the whole pub. *"The Master"*, who had noticed the fear of his apostles, came closer to them bringing with Him an aura of peace; he sat among them and spoke:

- *Peace be with you all!*

Hearing these words, *Peter* "Stone", *John* "The Younger", *Matthew* "The Taxman", *James* "The Older", and the other Apostles, recognized Him and were overjoyed. Then *"The Master"* turned towards *Thomas* the Apostle, known to them all as

"The Twin", and said to him:

- *Put your finger here and see my hands. Take your hand and put it in my side, and be not faithless, but believe.*

Then Thomas falling down before The Master exclaimed,

- *My Lord and my God!*

* * *

ABOUT THE AUTHOR

Michael Surmont is an Architect and Maths Teacher who enjoys creating short stories in which history and mystery collide in unpredictable ways. You will find more of his titles at:

CPSIA information can be obtained
at www.ICGtesting.com
Printed in the USA
BVHW031044191221
624455BV00007B/531